W9-AON-829

08/2020

PALM BEACH COUNTY
LIBRARY SYSTEM
3650 Summit Boulevard
West Palm Beach, FL 33406-4198

Max
and
Zoe

Celebrate Mother's Day

by Shelley Swanson Sateren

illustrated by Mary Sullivan

PICTURE WINDOW BOOKS
a capstone imprint

Max and Zoe is published by Picture Window Books
a Capstone Imprint
1710 Roe Crest Drive
North Mankato, Minnesota 56003
www.capstonepub.com

Library of Congress Cataloging-in-Publication Data
Sateren, Shelley Swanson.
Max and Zoe celebrate Mother's Day / by Shelley Swanson
Sateren; illustrated by Mary Sullivan.
p. cm. -- (Max and Zoe)
Summary: Max is planning to surprise his mother with breakfast
in bed on Mother's Day, but he does not know how to start the
stove.
ISBN 978-1-4048-6214-2 (library binding)
1. Mother's Day--Juvenile fiction. 2. Mothers and sons--Juvenile
fiction. 3. Cooking--Juvenile fiction. [1. Mother's Day--Fiction.
2. Mothers and sons--Fiction. 3. Cooking--Fiction.] I. Sullivan,
Mary, 1958- ill. II. Title. III. Series: Sateren, Shelley Swanson. Max
and Zoe.

PZ7.S249155Mcm 2012
813.54--dc23

2011051235

Designer: Emily Harris

Printed in the United States of America.
062019   002307

Table of Contents

Zoe ran over to Max's apartment.

"Did you get everything?" Max whispered.

"Yeah," Zoe said. She pointed at her backpack. "Everything is in here."

"Perfect!" whispered Max. "You're the best!"

"Thanks, Max," said Zoe.

"Quiet," whispered Max. "We don't want my mom to hear us. It has to be a total surprise!"

Zoe took the pancake mix out of her bag.

Max read the box.

"I've made these with Mom.
I did most of it. Well, except
for one part," he said.

"What part?" Zoe asked.

"Turning on the stove. She wouldn't let me. But tomorrow morning I'll do it," Max said.

"That doesn't sound like a good idea, Max," said Zoe.

"But if Mom comes into the kitchen, it won't be breakfast in bed," Max said.

"You don't want to make your mom mad on Mother's Day," Zoe said.

"Well, I'm not going to ruin the surprise," Max said.

Chapter 2
Being Sneaky

Zoe took a rose out of her backpack. "Go get a vase and fill it with water," she said.

"I can't! Mom is in the kitchen," Max said.

"Forget the vase," said Zoe. "Just get a glass of water."

Max left and came back with the glass.

Zoe put the rose in the water. Max hid the flower in his closet.

Zoe read the pancake box.

"Go get a big bowl," she said.

"What if Mom sees me?"
Max asked.

"Tiptoe past her," Zoe said.
"You have to be sneaky."

"I'll try," Max said.

Max peeked into the kitchen. Mom was washing dishes.

Max crawled under the table and across the floor.

He got a bowl. Suddenly, Buddy charged and jumped on Max.

"What are you doing with that bowl?" Max's mom asked.

"Um. Playing cars! The bowl is my steering wheel," Max said.

Mom smiled.

"Zoom!" Max drove away.

"That was close!" Max said as he hid the bowl under his bed. "But I was sneaky!"

"Now you should have everything you need," said Zoe.

"I hope so," Max said.

"I want this to be special for

my mom."

"It will be. Good luck,"

Zoe said.

Chapter 3
Breakfast in Bed

The next morning, Max and Buddy tiptoed to the kitchen.

Max put the rose, a plate, and a napkin on a tray. He made the pancake batter and got a pan.

"I'm ready to cook!" he said.

Buddy wagged his tail.

Max looked at the stove.
"When it's on, there's a blue
flame. What if I make the fire
too big?"

Buddy covered his head.

"Yeah. Scary. I think I need Mom's help," Max said.

Buddy hung his head.

"That means no breakfast in bed for Mom," Max said. "Wait! I have an idea!"

Max brought a pillow and some blankets to the kitchen. Buddy helped.

Then Max made a bed on the kitchen floor.

Max and Buddy ran to Mom's room.

"Happy Mother's Day!"
Max said.

"Thank you!" she said.

"Follow me," he said.

Max took Mom to the
kitchen.

"Get in, Mom. Breakfast in bed!" Max said.

"What a wonderful surprise!" his mom said.

"Can you start the stove first?" Max asked.

"I sure can," she said.

Then she climbed into her new bed.

Soon, Max served Mom breakfast in bed.

"These are wonderful!" she said. "Here, Buddy. Try one."

Buddy barked.

"He loves it," said Max.

"And I love you," Mom said with a smile.

"Happy Mother's Day, Mom!" said Max.

About the Author

Shelley Swanson Sateren is the author of many children's books and has worked as an editor and a bookseller. Today, besides writing, she works with children aged five to twelve in an after-school program. At home or at the cabin, Shelley loves to read, watch movies, cross-country ski, and walk. She lives in St. Paul, Minnesota, with her husband and two sons.

About the Illustrator

Mary Sullivan has been drawing and writing her whole life, which has mostly been spent in Texas. She earned her BFA from the University of Texas in Studio Art, but she considers herself a self-trained illustrator. Mary lives in Cedar Park, a suburb of Austin, Texas.

Glossary

batter (BAT-ur) — a mix of milk, eggs, and flour used in baking

pancake (PAN-kake) — a thin, flat cake made from batter and cooked in a pan

ruin (ROO-in) — to spoil something

tiptoe (TIP-toh) — to walk very quietly on the tips of your toes

tray (TRAY) — a flat container used to carry things

vase (VAYSS) — a container used to hold flowers

Discussion Questions

1. What important kitchen rule did Max almost break? Why are rules important?

2. If you could make one meal for your mom, what would it be? Why?

3. Max made Mother's Day special for his mom. How would you make Mother's Day special for your mom?

Writing Prompts

1. Write a letter or poem to your mom and give it to her.

2. It's important to follow rules so you stay safe. Make a list of five rules in your house.

3. Zoe helps Max with his big surprise. Write about a time when you helped a friend.

Make Your Own Pancakes

In the story, Max makes pancakes for his mom. You can make pancakes, too. Be sure to have an adult help you.

What you need:

- pancake batter (choose a box mix that says "just add water")

- water (enough to make the recipe on the box, plus 1 tablespoon more)

- a squirt bottle (such as a clean, empty chocolate syrup bottle) or a turkey baster

- a fry pan or griddle

- cooking spray

- spatula

- fresh berries

- maple syrup

What you do:

1. Follow the directions on the pancake box, and make the batter. Add an extra tablespoon of water.

2. Fill the squirt bottle or turkey baster with the batter.

3. Heat the pan and spray it with cooking spray.

4. With the squirt bottle or turkey baster, make fun shapes on the hot pan. (To make a heart pancake, squirt a V shape. The batter will spread out into a heart.)

5. Flip the pancakes when they are brown.

6. Serve them with maple syrup and fresh berries on top. Enjoy!

The Fun Doesn't Stop Here!

Discover more at www.capstonekids.com

- Videos & Contests
- Games & Puzzles
- Friends & Favorites
- Authors & Illustrators

Find cool websites and more books like this one at www.facthound.com. Just type in the Book ID **9781404862142** and you're ready to go!